THE WISHING WELL GHOST

TERRY DEARY

ILLUSTRATED BY
CHARLOTTE FIRMIN

A & C BLACK • LONDON

Black Cats

The Ramsbottom Rumble • Georgia Byng
Calamity Kate • Terry Deary
The Custard Kid • Terry Deary
The Ghosts of Batwing Castle • Terry Deary
Ghost Town • Terry Deary
Into the Lion's Den • Terry Deary
The Joke Factory • Terry Deary
The Treasure of Crazy Horse • Terry Deary
The Wishing Well Ghost • Terry Deary
A Witch in Time • Terry Deary
Dear Ms • Joan Poulson
It's a Tough Life • Jeremy Strong
Big Iggy • Kaye Umansky
Something Slimy on Primrose Drive • Karen Wallace

First paperback edition 2002
First published in hardback 1983 by
A & C Black Publishers Ltd
37 Soho Square, London W1D 3QZ
www.acblack.com

Text copyright © 1983 Terry Deary
Illustrations copyright © 1983 Charlotte Firmin
Cover illustration copyright © 2002 Chris Mould

The rights of Terry Deary and Charlotte Firmin to be identified as
author and illustrator of this work have been asserted by them
in accordance with the Copyrights, Designs and Patents Act 1988.

ISBN 0-7136-6201-8

A CIP record for this book is available from the
British Library.

A & C Black uses paper produced with elemental
chlorine-free pulp, harvested from managed sustainable forests.

Printed and bound in Spain by G. Z. Printek, Bilbao.

The Clinking

Billy Sunday gazed through his bedroom window. He looked over the moon-bright garden to where the black fence cast even blacker shadows.

'Clink!'

There it was again. That noise. He had thought he'd heard it last night and had sat up in bed to peer past the thread-bare curtains. But then it had started to rain; the moon was swallowed by a cloud and the pattering drops drowned the noise.

'Clink!'

But not tonight. It was clear enough – like the village blacksmith's hammer on his anvil from a long way away. But Billy knew the blacksmith was asleep. And there was something about the sound that made him feel it came from closer at hand. From the bottom of the garden to be exact.

But he couldn't see anything. The moon dazzled him.

He closed his eyes and a hundred silver moons danced before them. He tried to picture the garden. What lay in the shadows?

Granny's shed.

That was where she brewed her rhubarb wine. Was that it? The clink of bottles? Was someone trying to steal Granny's wine – Granny's precious wine that she sold to make the money that kept her!

Billy was small for his age; he couldn't have done much against a fully grown burglar, but that didn't bother him. He was angry! He was furious!

How dare they rob his granny!

He swung his feet out of bed and he shivered as they touched the polished wooden floor. He tiptoed across to the door. 'Don't make a noise,' he thought. 'No need to wake Granny and worry her.'

A floor-board creaked. Billy held his breath. He reached for the door handle. The old door groaned. Billy bit his lip and listened for sounds of stirring in the next room. All he heard was the scuttering of mice in the rafters, like the patter of rain on dead leaves. And a gentle snore from Granny.

Then, 'clink!'

The boy crept downstairs, through the kitchen and out of the back door. The silver-green grass tickled Billy's feet as he slid over the lawn.

When he reached the shed he gripped the window-ledge and raised his nose above the window sill. He looked into the window . . . two eyes stared back at him.

Billy's heart seemed to stop for a moment.

He blinked.

The eyes blinked!

He raised his chin a little and the face at the window raised its chin.

Billy smiled weakly . . . and the face smiled back. Then Billy grinned when he realised he was looking at his own reflection in the glass. He rubbed the window and tried to look into the dark shed.

He could see nothing. If someone was in there, they must be working without a light and without a sound.

Then . . . 'clink!'

Billy swung round. The sound had come from behind him – from the opposite corner of the garden. But it couldn't have done . . . there was nothing there! Just a deep, dark hole in the ground!

Billy fled.

Across the grass, through the kitchen, up the stairs and into bed. As he pulled the covers over his head and shivered in the warm dark, Billy remembered the story which Granny used to tell him when he was younger.

She said the hole in the ground was haunted! As Billy had grown up, he began to think that his granny had told him the story to keep him away from the dangerous spot. He had almost forgotten the story about the ghost... until tonight!

For, if it wasn't a ghost... what was it?

2

Quintus Quigley

Billy woke from a restless sleep. The rising sun lit the sky with a rose-gold glow. The boy rubbed his eyes and stared hard at the garden. His fears melted with the morning mist.

There was nothing to be afraid of . . . just a hole in the ground.

No, 'clink!' Then a clatter and a sizzle. That was just Granny making the breakfast.

The smoky smell of bacon tickled Billy's nose and made him hungry. He jumped out of bed, dressed quickly, washed and trotted downstairs.

'Do you always get up so early, Granny?' he yawned, as he entered the kitchen, warm-scented with wood-smoke.

'Go to bed with the lamb and rise with the lark, as my grandad used to say,' Granny replied, cracking an egg into the pan with one hand. 'You're just in time,' she went on.

As Billy chewed his breakfast thoughtfully, he asked, 'Granny, is there really a ghost in the hole at the bottom of the garden?'

The old lady's eyes twinkled over her teacup. 'A ghost! Whoever gave you that idea?'

'You did!' Billy exclaimed. 'The first time I came to spend a summer holiday with you.'

'Oh, but you know what an old fibber I am,' she sighed.

Billy rested his chin on his hand and thought hard. 'If there isn't a ghost . . .' he began slowly.

'Ah! I didn't say there *isn't* a ghost,' Granny said quickly. 'My old grandad always used to tell me there *was* a ghost. But maybe he only said that to stop me going too near that old hole and falling down it.'

'So, why did you tell me?' Billy asked.

'To keep you from going too near, of course!' Granny replied.

Billy groaned. It was all very confusing. He was still trying to work it out, when there came a sharp rap on the front door.

Billy jumped to his feet and padded along the passage. He swung open the door to find himself staring at three brass buttons. The buttons were attached to a white coat . . . and the white coat was worn by one of the tallest men Billy had ever seen. The boy cricked his neck as he looked up to see a face even whiter than the coat – a face the sickly colour of boiled fish.

The hair on top was wild and wintry and as wispy as a dandelion seed. But the eyes were the

most frightening of all – for Billy couldn't see
them. They were hidden behind the two smoked
glass discs that made up the man's spectacles.

'Good morning. I'm Quintus Quigley, your
friendly local grocer,' the man said, and his voice
was as harsh as a crow with a sore throat. 'Who
are you?'

'I'm Billy... Billy Sunday,' the boy said.
There was a silence. Billy felt the man was
waiting for him to explain what he was doing
there. 'I'm on holiday here... with my
granny.'

'So. You're Mrs Sunday's grandson. A sort of
grand-sun-day, eh?' Quintus Quigley joked.
His laugh sounded like the cough of a sick
ostrich.

Billy didn't laugh. In fact, Billy had taken a
strong dislike to this white drainpipe of a man.

'Where is the old witch?' the grocer hissed.

Billy turned red. 'Don't you call my granny a witch!' he cried, 'or I'll... I'll...'

'Or you'll *what*?' Quintus Quigley sneered.

'Or... or I'll punch you on the nose!' Billy shouted.

The pale man pulled back his grey lips to reveal even greyer teeth. 'You couldn't even reach my nose... shorty.'

'Then I'll punch you on your knee-caps!' Billy replied hotly, adding, 'fish-face!'

'Billy!' Granny said sharply, as she appeared in the passage. 'That wasn't a very nice thing to call Mr Quigley. Remember, politeness costs nothing, as my grandad used to say.' Billy turned red. He felt ashamed that his granny had caught him being rude to one of her visitors.

'But he said some nasty things about you,' the boy muttered, to excuse his shame.

'Sticks and stones may break my bones, but names can never hurt me,' the old woman replied. Squinting up at the tall man she went on, 'Besides, Mr Quigley doesn't look a bit like a fish. Fish are much better looking! He looks more like an under-cooked suet pudding. So, what do you want, pudding face?'

Billy gasped to hear his granny say such a thing, then he almost choked with laughter when he saw the grocer's reaction. Quintus

Quigley pinched his lips into a furious scowl; the end of his nose seemed to turn purple. 'I have come for my money,' the man said in a hoarse voice.

'You can have it tomorrow,' Granny said sweetly.

The reply seemed to catch the tall man off his guard. 'Tomorrow?'

'Tomorrow,' Granny repeated. 'Of course, as my old grandad used to say, tomorrow never comes!'

Before the grocer could put his furious reply into words, Granny closed the door firmly and stood with her back to it.

Billy was left breathless by the exchange. While he was thinking of a hundred and two questions he wanted to ask his granny, the old lady surprised him yet again by saying something completely curious.

'Ding, dong bell,
Sally's in the well.'

3

Billy's Wish

Billy repeated slowly what his granny had said. 'Ding, dong, bell, Sally's in the well... shouldn't it be Pussy's in the well?'

'No. Definitely *Sally*. That's what my old grandad used to say,' Granny murmured as she led the way back to the kitchen. She seemed to have already forgotten her argument with the tall man at her front door. Billy had not forgotten; there were still a lot of questions he wanted to ask about Quintus Quigley – but there were just as many he wanted to ask about Granny's curious rhyme.

'Why did your grandad say that?' the boy demanded.

Granny poured out a fresh cup of tea. 'I don't know . . . but your talking about the ghost reminded me of what grandad used to say, oh, it must be fifty years ago when I was a little girl.'

'About the hole in the bottom of the garden?' Billy asked eagerly.

'Yes. When he was warning me to keep away from it,' the old lady replied.

'So, the hole in the ground is a well!' Billy said excitedly.

'I suppose it could have been once . . . there's certainly no water there now.'

'And Sally must have been a girl who fell down it!' Billy went on. 'But what does "Ding, dong, bell," mean?' he asked frowning.

'It could be the church bell,' Granny said. 'In olden days they used to ring it to gather all the people of the village together in an emergency.'

'You mean if a girl fell down the well, and they needed everybody's help to get her out?'

'Ye . . . es,' Granny said slowly. 'Or . . .'

'Or what, Granny?'

The old lady shuddered and stared into her teacup. 'Nothing, Billy. You're too young.'

'Oh, people are *always* saying that to me!' he cried. 'How will I ever learn anything if you won't tell me?'

'That's true,' Granny admitted.

'So, why else would they ring the church bell?'

'For a funeral,' Granny said simply.

'Oh,' Billy said, a little disappointed. Then he said it again. 'Oh!' he cried. 'That's it! Sally's funeral! She must have died when she fell down the hole!'

'No need to look so pleased about it,' Granny grumbled.

'No. I'm pleased because that explains every-thing!' Billy said.

Granny nodded wisely. 'I suppose it does. The hole was a well. A girl called Sally fell down it, killed herself . . .'

'And became a ghost!' Billy said finally. 'So the well *is* haunted! It wasn't just another of your grandad's stories.'

'It doesn't explain everything,' Granny said.

'What do you mean?'

'It doesn't explain what the silly girl was doing near the well in the first place,' Granny said sternly. 'Mind you keep away from it, Billy.'

'I will, Granny,' the boy said, but he wasn't really listening. Now that his curiosity was almost satisfied on the problem of the well, his mind jumped to the other matter. 'Granny,' he said suddenly. 'What did that Quintus Quigley man want?'

Granny, who was still thinking about the well, took a few moments to think about the boy's question. 'Oh . . . eh? Mr Quigley? He wanted his sugar money.'

'Sugar money? What's that?'

Granny sighed. 'To make wine from my rhubarb I have to use a lot of sugar. I buy the sugar from Mr Quigley. When I sell the wine I pay him.'

'So, why don't you pay him now. Get rid of him?' Billy asked. He shivered slightly as he remembered the pale, sneering face at the door.

'Because I haven't any money, Billy. The last lot of wine turned out badly. I didn't sell a single drop . . . but I used up all the sugar and Mr Quigley still wants to be paid for it!'

'That's terrible!' Billy cried. 'But my dad will lend you the money . . .'

'No!' The old lady's lips pressed firmly together and she thumped the table till the

teacups rattled. 'I won't take charity from anyone!'

Billy felt he'd offended her. He went on rather timidly, 'Then what will you do, Granny?'

The old lady shrugged. 'Young Quintus Quigley says that if I don't pay him in two days he'll take something else instead. I suppose I'll have to let him. I don't want any debts. In this life you must expect nothing for nothing.'

'But what does he want that you could give him?' Billy asked, looking around the simple little kitchen. He could see nothing of value whatever.

'He wants part of my cottage,' Granny said.

Billy scratched his head. Why would the grocer want part of this crumbling cottage? 'Which part?' he asked.

'He wants a piece of my garden . . .' Granny said.

Suddenly, without Granny saying another word, Billy knew what Quintus Quigley wanted. 'He wants the bottom corner, doesn't he?' the boy asked.

Granny nodded. 'That's right! Though why anyone would want a dusty old hole in the ground is beyond me!'

Billy finished his second cup of tea in thoughtful silence then asked his granny if he could go out into the garden to play.

The morning sun warmed the rhubarb patch, but Billy didn't feel it. He was shivering with some unknown fear as he approached the hole at the bottom of the garden. Now that he looked closely, he could see the crumbling remains of what used to be a wall around the well. 'Funny,' he thought. 'Now I know what it is, it's *obvious* it's a well!' He peered down into the bottomless blackness. Even the warm daylight failed to brighten up the gloomy air.

Billy Sunday knelt by the old well and sighed. 'I wish I could do something to help Granny,' he murmured.

'You really ought to throw a coin in the well if you want your wish to come true,' said a voice. It was a girl's voice. It came from directly behind Billy.

The boy swung round. He gulped so hard that he almost swallowed his tongue.

For, standing behind him was no one . . . no one at all!

4

Sally

When Billy had recovered his breath and rubbed his eyes, he began to think he must have imagined the voice. He couldn't speak to an empty space; he would look foolish. So he whispered.

'Who said that?'

'I did!' came the reply as quick as a thought.

Billy gave a nervous laugh. He was looking at the spot where the voice had come from and he could still see nothing. Perhaps someone was playing a trick on him. 'Wh-where are you?' he asked quietly.

'Standing in front of you,' the voice replied.

'I . . . I can't see you.'

The voice gave a gentle sigh. 'No, I suppose you can't. It's very hard to make myself visible when the sun is shining . . . it takes a lot of energy. Come back tonight and I'll glow like a fire-fly.'

'You're the ghost!' Billy said, forgetting to keep his voice down.

'I suppose I am. My name is Sarah . . . but you can call me Sally. All my friends do,' the voice said cheerfully.

The rhyme ran through Billy's head once more. Ding, dong, bell; Sally's in the well.

'I'm Billy. I'm pleased to meet you . . . I think,' the boy said politely extending his hand.

The girl's voice giggled. 'Sorry, I don't have a hand to shake . . . to make a solid hand would take an *enormous* amount of energy. I'd have to rest for *hours* if I wanted to do that.'

'Oh . . . I see,' Billy said, feeling a little foolish with his hand hanging out like a puppet's. He felt he was about to blush so he quickly changed the subject. 'Did you fall down the well?' he asked.

Sally sighed again. 'Yes. Silly Sally, that's what they should call me!'

Billy suddenly remembered something his granny had said. 'What were you doing, to fall down the well?' he asked suddenly.

'Oh... being very wicked. I suppose what happened served me right!' the girl said in a sad voice.

'What happened?' Billy asked.

'I was fishing for money,' the girl said in a small, guilty voice.

'Money?'

'Yes the well was full of it!'

'It's a money well?' Billy asked.

'No, no, no. It's a *wishing* well,' the girl replied. 'People used to come here to make a wish. To make the wish come true you had to throw a coin down the well as you wished.'

'Did it really work?' Billy demanded.

'Sometimes,' Sally said gently. 'But it didn't always work the way you wanted it to! My family were poor. I took our last groat, threw it down the well and wished I were so rich I could lie on a bed of money. When nothing happened I went back to the well with a milk jug and a ball of wool . . .'

'You wanted to lower the jug down on the end of the wool and scoop up your money!' Billy cried.

'That was what I wanted at first . . . but with a bit of luck I hoped to scoop up much, much more. I was greedy, you see? But the wool was just too short – the well was very deep – and I could only reach the bottom if I leaned right over the edge.'

'You fell?'

'Of course! The well made my wish come true . . . I lay on my bed of money – at the bottom of the well!' Suddenly the voice laughed with a sound like the tinkling of coins. Billy Sunday shivered.

'And that's why you haunt the well,' he said, half to himself. 'The clinking of coins is your warning to others not to do the same as you!'

'What on earth are you talking about?' the girl's voice asked with a giggle.

Billy felt a little offended. He had thought himself so clever because he had solved the mystery of the clinking. Now this ghost-girl was making fun of him. 'Then why *do* you haunt the well?' he asked with a trace of a sulk in his voice.

'Oh, but I don't haunt the well,' she replied with a puzzled tone.

'I've heard you,' Billy said crossly. 'The last two nights. Clink, clink, clink. Last night I came down to investigate and I heard the sound coming quite clearly from the hole . . . I mean the well.'

'But that wasn't me!' Sally said.

'It must have been!' Billy insisted.

'It couldn't have been. For four hundred years I've been seeking this well,' Sally said and the boy noticed her voice was becoming fainter. 'I needed to find it to let my ghost rest. I found it at last . . . this morning.'

'Then if *you* haven't been haunting it, who has?'

'Don't know,' the voice replied weakly. 'Come back tonight . . . find out . . .'

'Where are you going?' Billy cried desperately.

'Away . . . no energy . . . tonight . . . after rest . . .'

'When?'

'Hour after sunset . . . must rest . . .'

'And will I be able to *see* you then?' the boy shouted.

'See me . . .' the voice said and the words were swept away by the soft morning breeze. 'See me, Billy . . . bye . . .'

And Sally was gone.

5

The Treasure Hunters

Billy was restless all day. He tried to read a book to calm his racing mind but, although he turned the pages, the words meant nothing. All he could think about was his next meeting with his new ghost-friend.

Granny thought that Billy must be ill . . . or worried about something. 'Care killed a cat,' the old lady muttered, and tried to take Billy's mind off his problem by giving him lots of things to do. No sooner had he finished peeling the potatoes for lunch than she sent him off to the baker's for bread.

But over lunch he was still unusually quiet. At last Granny said to him, 'A penny for your thoughts?'

Billy jumped. Had Granny read his mind? That was just what he'd been thinking about... throwing a penny down the wishing well and asking the well to help his granny. It's nothing, Granny,' he muttered with a weak smile.

'Remember, a problem shared is a problem halved,' Granny said wisely.

'Did grandad say that?' Billy asked.

'No. I did. So, if you've got something on your mind you could tell me . . . or if you don't want to tell me you can get out from under my feet. Go and play with Mr Bell the Butcher's boys, if you want a couple of friends your own age.'

Billy pulled a face. 'Oh, they're all right . . . it's just they never want to do anything exciting.'

Granny wagged a thin finger under Billy's nose. 'If by that you mean they never want to do anything that would get them into trouble, then you just remember this, Billy Sunday. He that seeks trouble never misses. So, be warned!'

Billy shrugged. 'It's not really that. It's just that I want to be by myself for a while. I have a lot to think about.'

'Right!' Granny said jumping nimbly to her feet. 'Take this,' she said tearing off a piece of bread from the fresh loaf. 'And this, and this . . . and this,' she went on passing him a broom handle, a reel of thread and a pin.

Billy looked at the collection a little stupidly. 'But what are these for?'

'What are these for? What are *these* for? Have you never made a fishing rod before?' Granny cried. 'Go on. Off you go. Down to the stream.'

Billy picked up the things and walked to the door a little more cheerfully.

'And mind you don't fall in!' his granny called after him.

'Don't worry,' Billy replied seriously, thinking of Sally and the well. 'I'll be very careful never to fall in anything!'

The stream was peaceful and Billy enjoyed his afternoon, even though the fish sniffed at his bait and swam off smirking. Still, the day dragged by. He was glad to slip into bed and watch the sun set in a smoky haze.

When the stars began to pepper the sky he crept out of bed and into the garden. The quiet, lavender-scented garden was as still as the dust at the bottom of the well. At first Billy moved to perch on the moss-covered wall around the dark pit, but the sight of the gaping black mouth made him giddy. It seemed to draw him like a magnet. It called to him voicelessly, 'Come along, Billy . . . let's play a game . . . see if you can take my treasure!'

He wanted to close his eyes to shut out the sight . . . he wanted to stop his feet which were dragging him closer and closer to the waiting mouth . . . but he couldn't.

'Billy!' A voice said suddenly.

The boy blinked and woke from his trance.

He turned and his face was moon-pale in the starlight.

'Billy! You were awfully close to the well. You're not ready to become a ghost just yet!'

He knew the voice . . . it belonged to a girl called Sally. But the figure which shone like satin was strange to him. The girl was about his own age and height, the face round and mischievous . . . just as he had imagined it might be. But the clothes were odd. Like something out of his history books.

'Sally?' he said carefully.

The girl grinned, took the full skirts in her hands and curtsied politely. 'At your service, Master Billy,' she said.

Billy bent his head forward in a clumsy bow because he imagined that was what was expected in reply.

Sally moved closer to him. She looked solid enough until she stood between the moon and Billy. Then the boy could see the glowing crescent shining through her. 'Shall we go ghost hunting?' she asked playfully.

'Er . . . yes,' Billy answered, still nervous.

'What time does your ghost usually start work?' the ghost-girl asked brightly.

'When the moon rises over that tree,' Billy said pointing to the poplar in the lane at the bottom of the garden. 'About eleven o'clock I think,' Billy said.

'That's odd,' Sally replied lightly. 'Most ghosts prefer to start work about midnight . . . the witching hour they call it.'

'Why is that?'

'I don't know. Some kind of old tradition, I think,' Sally said with a careless shrug.

Just then the peace of the garden was broken by two noises. The first was the distant chiming of the church clock, announcing to the village that it was eleven.

But the next was a stranger sound at first . . .
and more frightening. A scrabbling, scuffling,
scratching sound followed by grunting.

'Quick, behind that hut!' Sally hissed in
Billy's ear, before she snapped into invisibility
like an electric light bulb being switched off.

Billy scurried behind his granny's garden
shed and peered at the spot on the fence where
the sounds seemed to be coming from. Slowly
the figure of a man unwound its long length and
stood on top of the fence. Silhouetted by the
moon, he looked like a tall chimney with a
sweep's brush poking from the top. 'That would
be his wild hair,' Billy thought, for he had seen
that figure once before . . . and once seen, never
forgotten, as his Granny would say.

The man bent down and hauled something else onto the fence alongside him. It was about half the man's height but five times as broad. A barrel, Billy thought for a moment . . . until the 'barrel' stretched out two frantic, waving arms to keep its balance on top of the narrow fence.

A second man! As fat as the first man was thin.

For an instant, Billy saw the grotesque figures as a paintbrush and a paintpot on his granny's garden fence.

A second later the fat figure lost its balance and crashed into the garden with a squeaking scream.

'Funny sort of ghosts,' Sally's voice whispered in Billy's ear.

'That's because they aren't ghosts,' the boy replied. 'They're real live men, as solid as you and me... well as solid as me anyway.'

'You know them?'

'I've never seen the fat one... but the tall one is Quintus Quigley the grocer – and I'd give my granny's best teapot to know what he's doing here at this time of night!'

6

Septimus Sly

From his hiding place behind the shed, Billy could see and hear everything that was going on in the garden. The paint-brush figure of Quintus Quigley jumped up and down on its fence perch and croaked some dreadful oaths at his partner, groaning in the shadows. 'Septimus Sly!' he hissed, 'you are the fattest little . . . thickest little . . . most bean-brained little villain in this village. No. In the world!'

The grocer bent forward like a frayed pipe-cleaner and began again. 'You are . . . ohh!' He suddenly stopped. 'Ohhhhh!' he cried as his arms began to whirl like under-fed windmills. 'Ohhh-hhh-hhh!' came the desperate cry as he toppled off the fence.

'EEEK!' came a pained cry from below. 'Watch what you're doing, you clumsy stick of white rhubarb!'

'Don't you call me names, you over-stuffed sausage!' came the reply.

'You landed on my head!' the little man protested.

'That's my bad luck,' the other retorted. 'It's the only hard bit about you . . . bone head!'

'Chalk-face!'

'I told you not to call me names, you two-legged jelly-fish!'

'What you going to do about it then?'

'I'll sack you!' Quintus Quigley replied in the slow, nasty voice that Billy had come to know and hate.

'Can't sack *me*, you greasy string of spaghetti. I know too much about you and your evil schemes,' the little man answered, with satisfaction oiling his squeaky voice.

'We shouldn't be arguing like this, Septimus my dear friend,' the grocer said, suddenly smooth. 'Allow me to help you to your little fat legs.'

'What was that?' his partner said sharply.

'I said, allow me to assist you.'

The voices were quiet again. The argument was over as quickly as it had started and Billy had to strain to hear the men talking.

'What do we do tonight?' Septimus Sly asked.

'Well, I thought . . .' Quintus Quigley began.

'That's a good one!' The small man exploded with a cackling laugh. '*Well*, you said! Well! Wishing well! Get it!'

'No!'

'Never mind . . . get on with it.'

'I thought,' Quintus Quigley resumed, in a voice that was colder than a polar bear's paw, 'I thought that *you* could go down the well tonight!'

'Me!' Septimus Sly squeaked. 'Me? The hole's too narrow!'

'Or you're too fat,' the tall man muttered.

'What was that?'

'I said . . . fancy that!'

'Hmmph! Anyway, why don't you go down again?'

'We've tried that the last two nights. I can get down. The trouble is, when I reach the bottom I'm too tall to bend over and scoop up the coins. I just keep bashing my head on the side of the well,' Quintus Quigley explained. Billy had a feeling that the tall man was using all his patience to keep himself from losing his temper.

'So, why would I be any better?' Septimus Sly asked.

'You're so short you're already half-way there!' the grocer pointed out. 'Just a slight bend of your knees, stretch those long monkey-like arms . . .'

'What was that?'

'I said . . . stretch those long, muscular arms, and Bob's your auntie!'

'I suppose it's worth a try,' the small man admitted.

'You can't do worse than me!' Quintus Quigley pointed out. 'Two nights and we only have half a dozen items.'

'Yes. It's worth a try,' Septimus Sly repeated. 'And if it doesn't work?'

'If it doesn't work? Then it will have to be . . . Plan Two!' Quintus Quigley croaked and there was glee in his voice.

'Oh, yes,' his little partner giggled. 'Plan Two!'

Billy's mouth had gone dry. There was something about that evil chuckle and the way he had said 'Plan Two' that made Billy worried. Something told him that Plan Two was even nastier than this mean Plan One – stealing an old lady's treasure from under her nose . . . or at least from under her feet!

While the two men busied themselves with a rope, Billy whispered quietly into the air. 'Sally? Sally, are you there?'

'Yes,' the girl replied and slowly her form appeared. A rainbow mist at first, gradually taking on the shape of a phantom girl.

'What can we do?' Billy asked.

'I don't know. But we have to do something . . . and quickly!'

'You mean before they steal my granny's treasure?'

'No. I mean before they find my silver locket!' the girl said softly . . . and the fear in her voice made Billy shudder.

The Ghost's Story

Billy sat on the cool earth and rested his back against the wooden shed at the bottom of his granny's garden. 'I've been so worried about Granny,' he admitted, 'that I forgot you must have problems too. Why have you come back after four hundred years, to haunt the well? And why do you need your locket?'

The girl's ghost floated down to rest beside him. 'You don't know much about ghosts, do you Billy?' she said.

Something about the way she said it made her sound much older. Then he remembered: she might look like a girl of his age, but she was really over four hundred years old – and that was even older than his granny! 'I've never met a ghost before,' he admitted.

'Of course,' the girl said. 'Of course,' she murmured like an echo of her own voice. 'The first thing you have to understand is that ghosts aren't ghosts because they want to be ghosts . . . they're ghosts because they *have* to be ghosts. They're forced to wander the earth until they're laid to rest.'

'Weren't you laid to rest, then?' Billy asked.

'I don't think so. I couldn't have been or I wouldn't be here now, would I?' Sally said.

'No, I suppose not. But why? What went wrong?'

'I'll tell you what I think happened,' Sally said thoughtfully. 'I was sitting on the well one warm Autumn evening, fishing for money, when I slipped and fell in. I don't remember much. I must have bumped my head on the way down. When I came to, I was in what the ghost people call "Limbo". A world between worlds. Not this life – not the after-life.'

'What was it like?' Billy asked.

'I can't describe it . . . I mean it wasn't anything. It wasn't light yet it wasn't dark. There were no shapes, no sounds. It wasn't life and it wasn't death.'

'But why didn't you go on to that other world . . . the afterlife?'

'Because I had left something behind in this world. My body. It was never properly buried. Never laid to rest. So my ghost can never rest!' the girl explained.

Billy was startled and a bit uncomfortable. 'You mean . . . it's still at the bottom of the well?'

'Oh, no. That was four hundred years ago. It would have turned to dust years ago and drifted away,' Sally said. Billy gave a small gasp of relief.

'Why were you never buried properly?' the boy asked.

'I don't know. Maybe no one ever knew where I was; maybe they just couldn't think of a way to get me out. Anyway, there I was . . . and there I stayed.'

'What can you do about it?' Billy asked.

'I think I've found a way to lay my ghost to rest,' Sally said eagerly. 'I met a ghost in Limbo and he told me there is a way. I have to return to the spot where I lived, find something that belonged to me and give it a proper burial.'

'Then you will be free?'

'Then I'll be free!' Sally agreed. 'The only thing I can think of that may still be around is a gift that my aunt left in her will . . . something I was wearing on the day I fell down the well.'

'A locket!' Billy cried. 'I see! That's why you have to find it before those two men do!' Suddenly Granny's problem seemed small compared with the urgency of Sally's search.

'That's right . . . but I'll need some help,' the girl's voice said quietly.

'I'll help you. What can I do?' Billy said jumping to his feet.

'I haven't got much strength . . . you saw the way I faded away this afternoon just through talking too much.'

Billy nodded.

'Making myself appear to you takes even more energy . . . but to lift a silver chain up a well shaft and carry it all the way to the churchyard would be more than I could manage. I can lift small things for small distances – but that would be just too much.'

'Don't worry. I'll find your locket!' the boy said quickly. 'I'll borrow a rope and lower myself down . . . I'll take a torch . . . and I'll find that locket for you, Sally. Don't worry, I'll find it!'

'Oh, but you won't,' said a hoarse hissing voice over the boy's shoulder. He spun round to find himself looking into the milk-white face of Quintus Quigley. In the darkened garden the long face glowed like a lantern . . . but those dark circles of glass in front of his eyes looked as bottomless as the well itself. And when Quintus Quigley grinned, his head was as gruesome as the skull on a pirate flag.

'You won't find any locket down there if you search for a thousand years, will he, Septimus?'

The little man poked his head around the corner of the shed and Billy saw it clearly for the first time. A lumpy warted face like a toad.

'No you won't,' squeaked the toad-face. 'No you won't!'

'Tell him why!' chortled Quintus Quigley.

'Because you have it, Quintus . . . you picked it up last night!'

8

Partners in Crime

Billy had stood open-mouthed while the villains had gloated. Now he found his tongue. 'Get out of my granny's garden or I'll shout so loud everyone in the village will come and throw you out!' he said boldly bluffing.

'You open your mouth and we'll pop you down that well before you can say Septimus Sly. Isn't that right, Septimus?'

'That's right, Quintus,' the little man leered. 'Then there'll be two wishing well ghosts!' he said and gave a cackling laugh at his own joke.

'They can keep each other company . . . such a sad story about the little lost ghost,' sneered the tall man.

'You know the story?' Billy gasped.

'Of course we know it. We were standing just around the corner of the shed all the time she was telling it!' the grocer said with a wheezing laugh.

'You didn't exactly keep your voices down,' Septimus Sly put in.

'And we master criminals have ears like hawks . . . isn't that right, Septimus?'

'Pardon?'

'I said . . . oh, never mind. The point is we heard your story . . . and very interesting it was too. We can abandon Plan One!' Quintus Quigley said contentedly.

'What's Plan One?' Billy asked.

The tall grocer stroked his long chin and looked at the boy. 'I don't suppose there's any harm in telling you now,' he said.

'No harm at all,' his stout partner agreed.

'Plan One was to go down the well at night and recover all the coins down there. I was clearing out my stock room a month ago when I found an old map showing that the hole in the ground was in fact an ancient wishing well!'

For the first time Sally found the energy to speak. 'But why?' she asked. 'Why go to all that trouble for just a few pounds?'

Quintus Quigley turned his sneer upon the girl. 'Because, my faint phantom friend, you are forgetting something very important. The coins that were thrown down there are now over four hundred years old. They are not just coins . . . they are antiques. Rich men who collect such things will pay a king's ransom to have that little lot in their greedy hands.'

'Those coins belong to my granny!' Billy said angrily.

'I know that! That's why we had to steal them

in the dead of night!' the grocer snapped.
'Anyway, they wouldn't have been on your
granny's land for much longer... Plan Two was
just about to succeed!'

'Ah, yes, Plan Two!' Septimus Sly echoed,
rubbing his hands together with a sound like
sandpaper on grit.

'What is Plan Two?' Billy asked.

Quintus Quigley leaned forward and prodded
Billy with a bony finger. 'Wouldn't you just like
to know?'

'Not if it's as silly as Plan One,' Billy said
lightly.

The grocer spluttered for a moment. 'Silly!'
he exploded. 'Silly! Right, young man. I'll tell
you what it was and we'll see if it was *silly*!'

'Please yourself,' Billy said.

'Plan Two was to get your old granny to hand over the well to me! Once we owned it, we wouldn't have to scrabble around in the dark! We could simply dig up the whole lot till the hole was big enough for even Septimus Sly to walk in!'

'Watch it, Quintus!'

'Sorry Septimus. Plan Two was to wait until your granny's wine business failed and she got deeply in debt with us! That would be the signal for kind Quintus Quigley to release the old lady from her debts... in exchange for a dusty old hole in the ground. See?'

'There's nothing very clever about that,' Billy argued. 'Granny makes very good wine. How could you know when one lot would turn bad?'

'Because I supply the sugar!'

'So?'

'So . . . the last lot of "sugar" wasn't sugar at all . . . it was *salt*!'

Quintus Quigley threw back his head to roar with laughter . . . and that was just the opening Billy was waiting for. He rushed forward with a cry of fury and kicked the tall villain on the shin.

'Ha! Ha! . . . Ouch!' cried Quintus Quigley.

'Get him, Billy,' cried Sally.

'Look out, Quintus! . . . oh, good shot, son,' cried Septimus Sly.

'You get out of my granny's garden and keep your hands off my granny's treasure!' shouted Billy. Before the boy could take a second kick, the tall man grasped him cruelly by the hair and held him easily at arm's length.

'Listen here... oh, my shin... you stupid boy... oh, I think you've broken it... your granny can keep her rotten garden and her rotten money. Septimus Sly and I have bigger fish to fry!'

Billy stopped struggling. He listened sullenly while Quintus Quigley went on with a sneer. 'Now that we have your ghostly little friend to help us, we can go on to much greater crimes. The law may stop a man . . . but it cannot stop a ghost! Sally, my four hundred year old friend . . . you and I are going to be partners!'

9

The Plan

Billy stopped struggling with the tall grocer and pulled himself away from the man's grasp.

'What do you mean?' he asked suspiciously.

'Exactly what I say. You can keep your little hole in the ground. It was always a dangerous scheme. If we didn't break our necks getting the old coins to the surface, there was always the chance that the law would trace the money back to us. If they found out those coins were taken without your granny's consent... we'd have been in trouble!' Quintus Quigley explained.

'That's why Plan Two was better,' Septimus Sly squeaked. 'With Plan Two the money would have been on *our* land! A brilliant plan, Plan Two. Glad I thought of it!'

Quintus Quigley turned on him sharply. 'What are you talking about, you fat freak? *I* thought of it!'

'*I* did!'

'*I* did . . . look, what does it matter *who* thought of it. We're not going to use it. We're using Plan Three instead.'

Septimus Sly chuckled an evil chuckle. 'Oh, yes . . . hee-hee . . . Plan Three . . . hee-hee.'

'What are you laughing at?' the grocer hissed.

'At Plan Three, of course – it's so wicked!'

'How do you know? I haven't even told you what it is yet!'

The little man stopped laughing for a moment and thought about it. 'Well, Quintus, if it's one of your plans its *bound* to be wicked!' he declared.

'Ho-ho! That's true! That's very true!' Quintus Quigley chortled. For a minute the two men rocked with quiet laughter.

Sally coughed. 'Ahem, if you're going to involve me in this plan don't you think you should tell me about it?' she asked.

Septimus Sly wiped a happy tear from his eye and giggled, 'I suppose we should tell you, hee-hee!' He thought for a few moments then added a little more seriously. 'Come to think of it, Quintus, shouldn't you tell me?'

'If you'll stop your **giggling** and listen, I will!' Quintus Quigley snarled.

'What about the boy?' the small, fat man asked with a nod in Billy's direction.

'He doesn't matter,' his tall partner sneered. 'If *we* don't tell him, it's for sure his little spooky friend will sooner or later. Anyway . . . perhaps he can be useful to us!'

'Me? Help you! Why should I?' Billy demanded.

'Because if you don't, your little girl friend will *never* get her locket back . . . her ghost can wander the earth for evermore!' Quintus Quigley snapped.

'That's right, you tell him!' Septimus Sly jeered.

'Please do as he says!' Sally groaned. Then, in a voice so gentle that only Billy could hear she went on, 'We can think of a way out of it later.'

Billy gave a nod that showed Sally he had heard. Then he said, aloud to the villainous pair, 'Very well . . . for Sally's sake, anything you say.'

'Sensible little boy,' Quintus Quigley hissed. 'Let us retire to my headquarters and I will explain Plan Three to you.'

'Where are your headquarters, Quintus?' Septimus asked.

'The back room of my shop, you fool!' the grocer snarled.

'Oh, well why didn't you say that in the first place?' his assistant said mildly.

'Because it is only the back of my shop when I'm being a grocer. When I am being a master criminal, it's my headquarters – understand?'

'I'm not stupid,' Septimus Sly said in a hurt tone.

'Then why do you act stupid?'

'Who says I act stupid?'

'I do!'

'I don't!'

'You do!'

And so the argument went on as Quintus Quigley led the way through the moon-shadowed lanes to the neatly whitewashed shop on the village green.

Quintus Quigley took a huge bunch of keys from his belt and opened two locks and three padlocks before he opened the door a crack. Sliding his hand inside he flicked off a burglar alarm. The grocer turned and smiled. 'You have to be careful,' he said knowingly. 'There are a lot of thieves about!'

'True,' Billy muttered.

The grocer led the curious group past packets of tea and sacks of sugar and barrels of biscuits and tins of treacle and jars of jelly-babies.

The small back room was stacked to the ceiling with boxes and crates with labels like:

HANDLE WITH CARE

and

THIS WAY UP

Quintus Quigley flicked the dust off four orange crates and placed them in a circle. 'Sit down,' he ordered the other three. Billy and Septimus Sly obeyed – Sally chose to float. 'Now!' the white-faced man declared. 'Plan Three!'

10

The Gang of Four

Quintus Quigley took off his dark glasses and rubbed his eyes. When he looked up, Billy gave a startled blink. The tall grocer had pink eyes – rather like a white rabbit Billy had once seen.

'That must be why he wears the glasses,' Billy thought. 'Strong light hurts his eyes. I suppose that's why he enjoys creeping around at night, too!' Billy yawned. He had no idea what time it was, but he felt he should have been asleep hours ago.

'Plan Three!' the grocer chuckled again, and his eyes sparkled gold and pink in the candle-light. He looked around at the other three. Billy looked a little dazed with tiredness while Sally's faintly glowing face showed a curious smile of wise contentment.

Septimus Sly looked bored. 'For goodness sake, Quintus, get on with it!'

The white-haired man ignored the spiteful remark and took his time. He leaned back on his orange-box till his head rested against a case of dried prunes. At last he said slowly, 'We, my friends, are going to rob the midsummer fair!'

Billy just blinked again – he didn't know what the grocer was talking about.

Septimus Sly gasped, 'The midsummer fair!' and rolled his eyes in horror. 'You mean to tell me that your great plan is to rob a *fair*! You want to take a few pitiful pennies from a bunch of beggarly brats?' He threw his hands in the air. 'Lor' help me! Why not just pinch my piggy-bank and get it over with?'

The grocer curled his grey lips back in a vicious sneer. 'Have you any idea how much those "beggarly brats" spend at the midsummer fair, my fat and foolish friend? Well? Have you?'

'Pennies,' Septimus Sly muttered, but he didn't sound so sure of himself now.

Quintus Quigley shook his head as though he felt sorry for the little man. 'You couldn't be more wrong!' he said with a quiet smile that twisted his face. 'Every snivelling child begs every last penny off his parents for the mid-summer fair! Thousands come from miles around and stay until they have no more to spend! They spend it on the roundabouts and the swings and the coconut shies . . . they spend it on the shooting gallery, the lucky dip and the roll-a-penny . . . then they go and beg more money from their kind mummies and daddies to fill their filthy faces with hot-dogs and toffee-apples and candy-floss . . .'

'I like candy-floss,' Septimus Sly put in wistfully.

'But you like money even more, don't you?'

The fat man nodded.

'And after we've robbed the fair, we'll have enough money to buy a hundred candy-floss machines!'

'You can't go from stall to stall pinching the money,' Billy objected. 'The constable would be called to arrest you before you reached the third stall!'

Quintus Quigley laughed. 'Of course he would. Do you think I don't know that? Who said anything about robbing the stalls? No one replied, so the grocer went on smugly, 'I plan to wait till all the money is collected together... and take it all at once!'

'How, Quintus?' Septimus Sly asked eagerly. There was no mockery in his voice now.

'Listen to a master-criminal, and find out,' Quintus replied. 'The showmen keep the loose change in their trailers for the next day . . . but they give the paper money to the fairground manager.'

'What is "paper money"?' Sally asked.

'The same as metal money . . . only . . . only . . . paper!' the grocer said impatiently. 'As I was saying, when the fair closes at midnight it is too late to go to the bank so the manager keeps it in a special trailer.'

'You mean like a big piggy-bank on wheels?' Septimus Sly asked and he licked his lips at the thought. 'All we have to do is tow it away!'

'Hmm. They aren't that stupid. It's surrounded by the other trailers. There's no way anyone could tow it out,' the pale grocer replied.

'So, we just break into it!' Septimus Sly suggested.

'No. It's made of steel as thick as your wrist. There is only one door. It has an unbreakable lock . . . and there is only one key, which the manager keeps under his pillow at night.'

'Then how *do* we get in?'

'I was coming to that! There is a small window. The glass is unbreakable and it's fastened on the inside . . . the only way to get the money out is to unfasten the window on the inside and pass the money out!'

Septimus Sly sighed. 'But, Quintus, how do you get *in* to unfasten the window?'

The grocer gave a slight smile and turned his eyes on Sally's calmly floating shape. 'There's only one way . . . you have to be able to walk through walls!'

Septimus Sly turned and looked at the girl too. 'I see! Oh, that's clever, Quintus . . . hee . . . heeee! Oh, that's very clever!'

While the two men chuckled heartily Billy asked quietly, 'How do you know all this, Mr Quigley?'

The smile vanished from the grocer's face and his eyes slid nervously around the room. 'I er, I . . . I used to work in the fair many years ago . . . before I became a grocer.'

'Really, Quintus?' his chubby colleague said. 'I didn't know that! What was it that you used to do in the fair?'

For the first time Billy saw some colour come to the cheeks of the grey-faced grocer. 'Never mind what I used to do, Septimus. That's not important. What matters is what I know!'

The small man shrugged his shoulders. 'Whatever you say, Quintus.'

'That's right,' the other man said harshly. 'Whatever *I* say. And I say I'm going to make that fair *pay* for the time I spent there.'

There was silence in the dusty stockroom.

No one knew quite what to say. Billy looked at the flickering candle shadows... then noticed that Sally had no shadow at all!

'It won't work,' the ghost-girl said.

The grocer slipped on his glasses and stared at her faint form. 'Why not?' he demanded.

'I may be able to find the energy to form a solid hand that could open a window catch . . . but I would never have the strength to carry bags of money through the window!' she explained softly.

Quintus Quigley grinned his ugly grey grin. 'You wouldn't have to! That's where my plan is so perfect. All you have to do is open the window. Granny's darling little boy will do the rest!' he said, jerking a thumb in Billy's direction.

'Me!' Billy exclaimed, suddenly coming wide awake.

'Of course! The window is too small for Septimus or me. You'll have to do it.'

'Why should I?' Billy said angrily.

'Because, if you don't, your ghostly girlfriend won't get her locket back,' the grocer hissed.

Billy bit his lip and remembered his promise to Sally. Finally he said. 'Very well. I'll help you. But I want Sally's locket.'

Quintus Quigley laughed harshly. 'Ha! When the money is safely in my hands . . .'

'*Our* hands,' Septimus Sly put in quickly.

'Exactly. When the money is safely in *our* hands, then you may have the locket!'

'Agree, Billy,' the girl whispered, drifting closer to the boy's ear.

'I agree,' Billy mumbled.

'Good!' Quintus Quigley said briskly. 'Billy, allow me to welcome you to my gang!'

'*Our* gang, Quintus!'

'Oh, shut up, chubby-chops!'

11

Midsummer Day

After the midnight meeting with Quintus Quigley, Billy slipped away to the village green for another talk with Sally. On a seat overlooking the star-speckled duck pond the ghost girl talked till she was as faint as a wisp of marsh-mist and her voice the shadow of a whisper. Her plan was a good one, but it still involved Billy going through with the robbery . . . and that was what worried him.

Still, he slept well and rose late the next morning. He picked moodily at his breakfast while Granny busied herself with a tub of rhubarb that gurgled and hissed on the open fire.

'Granny,' Billy said at last. 'Don't worry about Mr Quigley . . . about the money you owe him, I mean. It's going to be all right.'

'Lor' love you, child. I'm not worried about poor Mr Quigley!' she chuckled.

Billy's fork fell with a clatter to the plate. 'Poor!' he exclaimed. 'Poor! Why, Granny he's a horrible man . . . he's the nastiest man I've ever met!'

For the first time in his life Billy's granny spoke to him sharply. 'I won't have you saying that about the poor man, Billy!' she said.

Billy's mouth dropped open in surprise and confusion. 'A closed mouth catches no flies!' the old lady said sternly. Then, seeing the boy looked hurt, she sat at the table facing him and patted his hand. 'Listen, Billy . . . if people are wicked or nasty towards you then you have to ask yourself, why are they like that?'

'Well, I suppose he's always been like that,' Billy mumbled miserably.

'And you'd be wrong!' Granny said. 'When he was a boy of your age he was quiet and very shy. But as he grew older, he grew taller and thinner and *different* from all the other children. That white hair of his didn't help either. The other children started to make fun of him . . . when he lashed out at them they ganged up on the poor lad. Chased him through the streets . . . threw mud at him, called him names. As my grandad used to say, a mob has many heads, but no brains. So *of course* young Quintus became nasty . . . it was enough to make a saint turn nasty.'

'That's still no reason why he should take it out on you,' Billy argued.

'True, true. Two wrongs don't make a right,' Granny nodded. 'But it's not for the likes of me and you to set things right now. That young man has gone too far for that . . . one of these days he's going to do something *really* criminal . . .'

Billy's heart jumped. Did Granny know about the robbery? She couldn't. Should he tell her now? No. She would stop him going ahead with the plan and Sally might never get her locket back. 'How do you know, Granny?' he asked carefully.

'Because I've seen him with that wicked little Septimus Sly . . . thick as thieves they are. Made for each other, of course. Quintus has suffered all his life with people calling him cruel names . . . now he has someone just as unfortunate as him, that *he* can mock.'

Billy's mouth went dry. It was uncanny the

way the old lady knew things like that . . . almost as if she had heard the two men together as Billy had. If she knew that, what else did she know?

'What will happen to Mr Quigley?' he asked.

'He'll be caught,' Granny said quietly.

'But Granny,' Billy cried, 'how do you *know*?'

Granny smiled her old wise smile. 'Always remember, Billy, what is done by night appears by day.'

The boy jumped to his feet. It was too much for him. 'She *must* know!' he thought desperately. 'What is done by night,' she had said!

'Can I go and see the fairground being set up, Granny?' he asked.

'Of course you can!' Granny said cheerfully. She stood up and returned to the bubbling pot. 'The day is short and the work is long,' she said.

'Not today it isn't,' Billy replied. 'It's midsummer day . . . the longest day of the year.'

'And even the longest day, like the longest road, has an ending. So, don't waste it . . . off you go!'

But as that day wore on, Billy began to think it would *never* end. He mooned around the village green while the fair people set up their stalls and booths and rides. He felt he had been watching for hours, but the church clock was only just striking twelve as he turned home for lunch.

In the afternoon he wandered down to the wishing well. Sally wasn't there of course. She had told him she would have to rest and gather up her energy for the night ahead. And the wishing well looked sinister that afternoon, cool and liquid . . . inviting him to jump in and shelter from the heat of the sun. Granny called him back into the house just as he was leaning over to look into the depths . . . just as Sally had done four hundred years before.

Granny sent Billy off on a search of the country hedgerows for wild strawberries. He worked hard and the time passed a little more quickly. Granny paid him for his efforts and he went off to the roaring, jangling fairground to spend it.

But his money was soon gone. Afterwards, he couldn't remember what he had spent it on. His mind was on his next visit to the village green . . . at midnight.

'I'm going to bed early, Granny,' he said yawning.

'That's a good idea. You look tired. One hour's sleep before midnight is worth three after. Goodnight, Billy, sleep tight!'

But Billy didn't sleep tight. He didn't sleep at all. He lay in bed watching the light fade from the sky and listening to the faint noises of music and laughter from the fairground. Slowly these sounds died too. He heard Granny climb the stairs to bed and peer around his bedroom door. Billy squeezed his eyes shut and pretended to be asleep.

The church clock struck eleven.

Granny snored gently.

Billy climbed out of bed and crept into the warm, midsummer night to commit his first . . . and his last . . . robbery.

12

Midsummer Night

The midsummer moon rose, huge and ivory-yellow. Billy looked up to see its bloated face grinning at him, leering at him: 'I know what you're up to,' it seemed to say.

The moonlight lit the candy-stripe colours of the fairground rides and the spangled saddles of the roundabout horses. Billy felt their glossy eyes twinkling at his back. 'We know what you're up to!' the red, open mouths hissed. Billy was scared. His legs were as limp as wet rags.

He didn't even have Sally for comfort. The ghost girl was silent and invisible, saving her energy.

Quintus Quigley stood, tall as a heron, listening. Septimus Sly's oil-black eyes slithered around the shadows, nervous. The only sound Billy could hear was his own heart thumping.

'All clear, Quintus,' the little man squeaked, and his tinny voice seemed to echo off the glittering walls like breaking glass.

Quintus Quigley gave a single nod of his sharp, heron-head and stalked off towards the circle of caravans. 'Septimus,' he whispered,

'You stay here. On guard. Just in case our little friend here has tried something sneaky . . . like going to the village constable!'

'I didn't!' Billy cried, and his voice sounded like a pistol shot. The grocer clamped a white-gloved hand over the boy's mouth. They stood for a minute, Billy scarcely able to breathe, while they waited for lights to appear and worried showmen to come running. Nothing. The caravans stayed silent.

'Stay here, Septimus . . . just in case,' the grocer repeated slowly. He took Billy by the scruff of the neck and pushed him between two caravans. There, in the open space in the middle of the caravan circle, stood the bank. Ugly, squat and square. More like a tank than a bank. 'You know what to do,' the tall man's voice grated.

Billy nodded. 'Sally?'

'Yes?' came the instant reply in his ear.

'That window, Sally. Can you open it?' he said pointing to a small glass square sunk deep in the cold grey walls.

'I'll try.'

As Billy watched the dark square, a faint hand appeared. Slowly the hand became clearer and more solid. The boy shuddered at the sight of a hand with no arm attached to it. The fingers twitched and Billy's mouth went dry. He didn't want to look yet he couldn't tear his eyes away.

The fingers gripped the window latch and tugged. It didn't move. The entire hand wrapped itself around the fastening and pulled. Still it didn't move.

Billy felt panic. What if Sally couldn't open the window? He wouldn't mind . . . but would Mr Quigley break his promise about the girl's locket?

Then Billy blinked in disbelief. Floating in the air, alongside the hand, there began to appear a hammer. Not a heavy claw hammer such as his father used. A wooden hammer . . . a mallet! That was the name. When the mallet was fully formed the hand grasped it and swung it sharply at the catch. With a light 'click' the catch flew off and the window swung open.

In an instant the hand vanished and then the mallet. Sally's voice was in his ear. 'There you are, Billy.' The voice was weak. Billy felt Sally had exhausted herself with the effort. Never mind, she would soon be free; it would all be worth it.

'Now. Your turn, young man,' the grocer croaked. Before Billy could catch his breath, Quintus Quigley had picked him up by his waist and thrust him towards the opening. Billy's shoulders stuck in the narrow window-frame, but the tall man just kept pushing. The boy gasped as the metal frame dug into his shoulders and he wanted to cry out. Just when he thought he could bear it no more, he popped through the gap like a dart from a blow-pipe.

Billy landed on his head in the terrifying dark. It took him a minute to find his feet. He rubbed his head and stood up shakily. A lighted torch suddenly appeared through the window and Billy took it from the white-gloved hand. The boy looked round the van. It was very small, because it was lined from floor to ceiling with steel shelves. Each shelf had a label and a bag. The label showed what type of money the bags held.

It was difficult for Billy to read the labels because his hand trembled as he held the torch. At last he made out the shelf that held the twenty-pound notes. He took down the heavy bag and fumbled it through the window. The only sound to show that Quintus Quigley had received it was a small sigh of pleasure.

The bag with the ten-pound notes was even more tightly packed and Billy had to struggle to lift it over the sill. Lastly he passed the two bags jammed full of five-pound notes. That was all Quintus Quigley wanted. A couple of bags for him and a couple for Septimus Sly to carry.

Billy passed out the torch and waited.

'Mr Quigley?' he called. There was no reply.

Then a sickening thought struck Billy. Now that the grocer had the money, he could leave Billy in the caravan. The boy could never squeeze out without help . . . he would have to stay there till he was found in the morning!

'Mr Quigley!' he called in a high, trembling voice.

'Hush, boy!' came the reply. 'I'm merely checking the bags. Don't be impatient!'

'I want to get out!' he cried.

'And so you shall!' The white gloved hand

appeared through the opening and Billy grasped it. Billy felt his arm was being torn from its socket as he was dragged back through the window . . . but he didn't mind. He had a sudden urge to get away from this place as quickly as possible.

He landed on his head again, but at least it was on grass this time. When he picked himself up, Quintus Quigley had already turned his back and was lugging the money bags after him.

'Mr Quigley!' Billy panted. 'The locket! Sally's locket! You promised!'

The tall man turned with an impatient sneer. 'As soon as I give you that locket, you can go to the police!'

Billy suddenly realised that the man didn't intend to give it to him. Perhaps he had always planned it this way. The boy's quick temper rose once more. 'If you don't give me that locket *now* I'll shout and shout until everyone in the fairground is awake . . . I won't *have* to go to the police!'

Quintus Quigley didn't seem too disturbed by the threat. 'You can have the locket, you miserable little boy . . . you can even go to the village constable. By the time you get to his house, wake the fat old man up and get him back here, I'll be miles away!' The tall grocer thrust a hand into his pocket and brought out a fine silver chain with an oval pendant. He threw it to the ground and turned away.

Billy bent down quickly, snatched up the locket and ran. He sprinted into a gap between the caravans and headed off in the direction of the constable's house.

Quintus Quigley laughed silently. He grasped the four money bags and made for the spot where he had left his little partner.

In the shadow he made out the form of a man. 'Here, Septimus,' he hissed, 'take these two bags.' Quintus Quigley selected the two bags with the five-pound notes and threw them at the man's feet.

The man stepped forward. He was wearing a dark suit with glimmering silver buttons. The tall helmet on his head made him even taller than the grocer.

'Quintus Quigley,' he said in a gentle voice, 'I arrest you in the name of the law!'

13

The Stolen Ride

Quintus Quigley's spidery legs carried him across the fairground in huge strides. He rushed past the policeman and was surprised that the officer made no attempt to stop him.

The heavy money bags crashed against his legs but he didn't mind. He wouldn't have let go if he'd been sinking in a shark-infested pool. He dodged around the coconut shy and made for the gap between the hoop-la and the miniature railway. As he rounded the swings he almost ran into a policeman.

Quintus skidded to a halt and turned back. Again the officer made no attempt to stop him . . . but the grocer was worried. There was something that he couldn't quite understand – that second policeman looked exactly like the first! Yet it couldn't have been the first . . . no one could have reached that spot before Quintus.

He sped around the roundabouts and groaned when he saw his way blocked by yet another policeman. 'How many are there? And where have they come from?' he thought furiously. 'And why do they all look alike?'

There was only one way open to him now . . . and that was a dead end.

Almost.

It was a showground building. There was no choice. He had to go in . . . and hope that it had a back entrance. Quintus dashed past the pay-box and found himself on a narrow railway track. A new idea struck him. He turned back and grinned when he realised there was no police-man in sight. The grocer reached into the pay-box and flipped a switch. With a low whine an electric motor whirred into life and a small two-seater train clattered into view.

Quintus Quigley threw the money bags onto one seat as the train drew alongside him, and jogged alongside it. Just as he was about to step inside, an unseen hand pushed a control in the pay-box. The train shot forward at twice the previous speed and left Quintus Quigley stumbling frantically along the track.

'My money!' he cried as he watched the train disappear through some black curtains and into the dark building. 'My mo . . o . . ney!' he screamed, beginning to tear out tufts of wild white hair. A sound behind him made him swing round. Another little train was chugging along the rails towards him. Quintus Quigley jumped to the side of the track, grabbed the train as it rattled past and swung his long legs into the passenger seat. 'Follow that train!' he roared. Obediently the train chuntered towards the black curtains.

The curtains brushed the grocer's face and he swatted them aside like flies. Once inside, the darkness was total. Quintus Quigley took off his dark glasses and peered ahead, hoping to catch a glimpse of the first train with its precious load.

Then, above the clatter of the train came a moaning sound, soft at first . . . then louder . . . then deafening. The grocer pressed his hands to his ears. Still the moaning drilled its way into his head. It sounded like a man . . . a man in absolute agony! Quintus Quigley saw a flash of light and looked up just in time to see a skeleton whisk past the train.

The moaning stopped suddenly to be replaced by cackling laughter. The grocer almost jumped out of the little train as a cold, damp hand brushed against his face. 'Where am I?' he cried and an instant later he seemed to have his reply. To the accompaniment of tortured screams, the devil appeared above the track. He looked just as the devil ought: two wicked horns, a pointed tail and a forked beard. His cruel face was bathed in a flickering red glow.

'That's it!' Quintus Quigley giggled nervously. 'I've died. All that chasing around the fairground gave me a heart attack! I died and this is . . . this is hell!'

The tall man cringed as he rushed towards the devil . . . but the devil let him pass without a glance.

The train hurried him on into the darkness and silence. He was just beginning to breathe again when a coffin loomed ahead of him lit by a sickly purple glow. As the front of the engine passed the coffin, the lid sprang open and a rubbery green body popped out to snatch at the passenger's head. Quintus ducked sharply, bumping his forehead on the edge of the cab.

'Ho . . . ho . . . hoo!' rumbled the deafening laughter.

The grocer lay back in shock, hardly caring what came next. 'I can't be any more shocked than I am now,' he sighed. But he could. For the next shape was a familiar one. It was a small wooden cubicle.

'The pay-box!' Quintus cried. 'I've gone round in a circle!' As he sped past the box he glimpsed a notice on the side. He only saw it for an instant . . . but in that instant everything became clear. The notice said GHOST TRAIN 20P.

Quintus Quigley laughed. He lay back in his seat and laughed till tears ran down his white cheeks. As the train hurried him back into the building he giggled. The skeleton rattled his bones at Quintus but the tall man just waved. The devil roared . . . while Quintus cried 'Yoo-hoo!' The coffin sprang its surprise at him but he just said 'Boo!' to the corpse and giggled. After all, there's nothing *really* frightening about a ghost train when you *know* it's a ghost train!

When the pay-box appeared a second time Quintus climbed to his feet and swayed, ready to jump onto the platform. All he had to do was stand there and wait for his train load of money to come round.

But again the unseen hand pushed the control in the box and the little train surged forward. Quintus was dumped back into his seat and he swore as he was swept back into the building.

He was not in a mood to enjoy his third ride. He frowned at the skeleton and waited impatiently for the devil to appear.

But when it did appear he sat up with a start. For the devil's face was suddenly familiar . . . and it hadn't had a policeman's helmet on the last time he went round!

'Quintus Quigley!' said the devil-policeman. 'I arrest you in the name of the law!'

Quintus shuddered and rubbed his eyes. 'I must be tired,' he muttered. 'I seem to be dreaming.' But he wasn't so sure when the coffin opened and a green-faced man, in a red robe and a judge's wig, asked 'How do you plead? Guilty or not guilty?'

'Not guilty!' Quintus shouted over his shoulder. He struggled to stand up for a desperate leap from the cab as he passed the platform. But he had lost his nerve, and the train hurtled past at full speed.

'Quintus Quigley . . . I arrest you in the name of the law!'

'Quintus Quigley . . . How do you plead?'

Before he knew it, the grocer had gone round another circuit.

The next time the policeman stood on the track directly ahead of the train. 'Quintus Quigley . . . I arrest you in the name of the law!' the policeman said calmly and he raised his hand, as though he was on traffic duty, to stop the train.

The train didn't stop.

Quintus squealed as the locomotive charged at the waiting policeman. He waited for the sickening thump of it hitting him.

But the thump never came.

The train passed straight through him.

'It's a ghost!' Quintus cried. 'A real ghost! All those policemen I saw in the fairground were just one miserable ghostly copper! I bet it's a friend of that wishing well ghost!'

And Quintus would have won his bet! The ghost of PC Plumpton had had a marvellous time chasing Quintus onto the ghost train ride . . . just as that charming little girl Sally had asked him to.

'You late-lamented men of the law can't get the better of Quintus Quigley!' the grocer screamed, as the ghost of Judge Justin Thyme leaned from the coffin again.

As the train rattled by the platform for the sixth time, Quintus Quigley jumped. He bounced bonily on the bare wooden platform and came to a painful halt at the pay-box.

Reaching inside, he turned the speed control until the cars were trotting gently along the track. At last the bags of money appeared and the grocer grabbed them gratefully.

He turned.

He stopped.

He found himself face to face with a tall man in a blue uniform with silver buttons. 'Quintus Quigley,' the man said. 'I arrest you in the name of the law!'

Quintus grinned cunningly. 'You don't fool me, you phantom flat-foot!' he hissed. 'You can't stop me either!' he added with a wild cackle.

'Can't I sir?' the policeman asked stolidly.

'No!' the pale grocer screamed. 'I can walk straight through you!'

'Mad! Quite, quite mad!' the policeman muttered to the small boy who stood at his side.

'Who's mad?' Quintus asked sharply. 'You tried to drive me mad . . . you and your ghostly friends. But it didn't work! I'm as sane as . . . why I'm as sane and sober as that judge in there!'

'I see,' the policeman said gently. 'So, there's a judge in the ghost train is there? Well he's not the only judge you'll be seeing. You're under arrest.'

'Get out of my way, you simple-minded spectre!' yelled Quintus. He placed his hand in the face of the policeman and pushed.

He was a little surprised when his hand didn't pass straight through the face of the policeman.

But, then, it wouldn't. Because he was pushing at the rather podgy, very angry and extremely solid face of the village constable.

'Quintus Quigley . . . you are also charged with resisting arrest and assaulting a police officer!' the constable added angrily, as he snapped handcuffs around the grocer's spindly wrists.

14

Goodbye

Billy Sunday struggled up the hill where the village church stood. After two hours of questions and explanations at the police station he was dizzy with tiredness. Still, before he could go to bed, he had one more duty to perform.

At last the boy reached the graveyard and sat wearily at the foot of one of the graves. It was the grave of his great-grandmother. Granny used to visit it and place flowers there every week. Sally was searching the graveyard for some trace of her family resting places.

It was still quite dark and Billy laughed quietly to think that he was no longer afraid of ghosts! As he looked over the snoring village, the sky began to lighten. Slate grey at first, then touches of oyster pink. The street lamps began to flicker out like lanterns in a breeze.

Billy yawned.

'I can't find any graves of my family,' Sally whispered in his ear.

Billy snapped awake and realised that he had been dozing. 'Oh! Can I help you look? What is the family name?'

'Don't you know?' the girl asked.

'No, you never told me,' Billy said.

'Promise you won't laugh . . . it's rather an odd name,' the ghost said shyly.

'I won't laugh! Your name can't be any odder than mine!' Billy replied.

'Well . . .' the girl said slowly. 'My family name is Sunday.'

'Of course!' Billy cried. 'Granny told me that cottage had been in the family for hundreds of years! The Sunday family! You must be my cousin!'

The girl giggled. 'I don't think so, Billy. More likely your great-great-great-great-great-great-aunt!'

Billy jumped to his feet. 'How would you like to rest *here*?' he asked, showing Sally the headstone of Mildred Sunday. 'With my great-granny.'

'That would be most satisfactory, great-nephew William!' Sally whispered with mock seriousness.

Billy scooped out a small hollow between the flowers and placed Sally's silver locket carefully in the place. As he covered it up he heard a long whispering sigh like a stirring of the branches in the graveyard elm. 'Thank you Billy . . . and goodbye . . .' the sigh said.

'You aren't going already, are you?' Billy asked in panic.

'I'm sorry, Billy, I have to . . . you've set me free . . . I can't stay any longer . . .'

Already the voice sounded half a world away.

'Won't I ever see you at the wishing well again?' Billy cried.

'Never, Billy . . . never . . . but think of me when ever you go there to make a wish . . . remember me . . .'

'I will,' Billy called to the empty air. 'I will!'

As he trudged wearily down the hill, Sally seemed already to be half real, half dream.

Billy slept late that morning. He woke from a dream of a rattling ghost-train ride to find Granny shaking him by the shoulder. 'Sorry to wake you, love. But today's the day you go home. Your dad will be here in an hour to take you home.'

Billy sipped a cup of tea and was more than ever convinced that he had dreamed the whole adventure. But, when he told Granny the story, the old lady nodded wisely and said, 'No. It wasn't a dream, Billy. The news is all around the village that Quintus Quigley was arrested last night.'

'You said he'd get into serious trouble one day,' Billy reminded her.

'Yes. And I should have known it would be with that fairground. It was his revenge, you see . . . not just the money,' Granny said thoughtfully.

'Revenge?'

'Yes. You remember I told you he suffered from the cruelty of children at school?' Billy nodded. 'What *really* made him bitter was discovering that the grown-up world can be even crueller!' Granny settled herself on Billy's bed and explained. 'When he left school he found no one would give him a job . . . until the fairground people came. They offered him a job in their "House of Wonders" – as the world's thinnest and the world's whitest man all rolled into one.'

'Did he accept the job?' Billy asked.

'Oh, yes. He imagined that people would come from far and wide to see him and wonder at him. He would become famous!'

'And did the people come?'

'Oh yes. But not to wonder. They came to point . . . they came to jeer . . . they came to laugh!' Granny sighed. 'Quintus never forgave them. Oh, he put up with it for a whole summer season and made enough money to start up his business . . . but he never forgot.'

'I suppose he felt let down,' Billy said in a troubled voice. 'And now I've let him down by spoiling his robbery.'

'No!' Granny said firmly. 'You were quite right. He forced you to break the law . . . and you had a duty to help your great-aunt Sally. And don't forget that he's the man who tried to rob your old Gran and steal the wishing well money. You can feel a little sorry for Quintus . . . but don't go breaking your poor heart over him.'

Billy brightened. 'That's true . . . some good came of it. You have the wishing well money – you needn't work ever again!'

'What!' Granny cried throwing up her hands in horror. 'What would I do with myself without my work? Don't you worry. I have enough – and enough, as my old grandad used to say, is as good as a feast. I'll just leave those wishes where they are. The people who made those wishes didn't throw in their money just to have it all snaffled up by a greedy old granny!'

Billy began to argue but he was interrupted by a friendly rattle on the front door knocker. 'Heaven help us all,' Granny moaned. 'That'll be your dad . . . and you still in bed! What *will* he say! You get dressed quickly while I give him a cup of tea,' the old lady said, as she bustled to the bedroom door.

Billy's tired body ached as he swung his feet reluctantly to the floor. Two goodbyes in one morning seemed too much to bear.

'Granny,' he sighed. 'Do I have to go? Can't I stay just a little longer?'

The old lady stopped at the door and turned to face him with a gentle smile. 'No, Billy. You've had an exciting time here with me this week . . . and I'm pleased. You've been happy. But trying to hold on to happiness is like trying to carry water in a sieve, I always say. Just you remember what my old grandad used to tell me: everything has an end – and a sausage has two.'